TWO PAIRS OF SHOES

TWO PAIRS OF SHOES

RETOLD BY

P. L. TRAVERS

ILLUSTRATED BY

LEO AND DIANE
DILLON

THE VIKING PRESS   NEW YORK

To Khaled Moustapha

L. & D. D.

First Edition
Text Copyright © P. L. Travers, 1976
Illustrations Copyright © Leo Dillon and Diane Dillon, 1980
All rights reserved
First published in 1980 by The Viking Press
625 Madison Avenue, New York, N.Y. 10022
Published simultaneously in Canada by
Penguin Books Canada Limited
Printed in U.S.A.
1 2 3 4 5 84 83 82 81 80

Library of Congress Cataloging in Publication Data
Travers, Pamela L. Two pairs of shoes.
Summary: Retellings of two Near Eastern folk
tales reveal how two pairs of shoes unwittingly
reflect the true character of the men who own them.
1. Tales, Near East. [1. Folklore—Near
East] I. Dillon, Leo. II. Dillon, Diane. III. Title.
PZ8.1.T69Tw   [398.2] [E]   78-3386
ISBN 0-670-73677-5

ABU KASSEM'S SLIPPERS

LISTEN TO THE STORY OF

Abu Kassem, the merchant, who was known throughout Baghdad not only for his riches and his parsimony but also for his slippers, which were the outward and visible sign of his miserliness. They were so old, so dirty, so patched and tattered that they were the bane of every cobbler in the city and a byword among the citizens.

Clad in this deplorable footwear and a shabby caftan, Abu Kassem would go shuffling through the bazaar, sniffing around for bargains. One day he happened on a collection of little crystal bottles which, after much haggling, he managed to buy quite cheaply. And then, with typical miser's luck, he came upon, at cut price, a large supply of attar of roses with which to fill the bottles. The bazaar was agog at this double stroke, and Abu Kassem, congratulating himself on his sagacity, decided to celebrate the occasion by paying a visit to the public baths.

There, in the dressing room, he met his old friend Hassan, who took him to task in the matter of his slippers. "Look at them, Abu Kassem! Even a beggar would throw them away! But thou with all thy stored-up riches refuse to part with the dreadful things!"

"Waste not, want not," said Abu Kassem. "There is still a lot of wear in them." And he took off the precious offending slippers and hurried into the bath.

But Fate had caught him in her grip, as we shall presently see. It so happened that the Cadi of Baghdad had also decided to bathe that day. Abu Kassem finished before him, put on his outer garments and turban, and felt about for his slippers. Where were they? They had disappeared. But in their place was another pair, shiny and bright and new. "Ah," said Abu Kassem. "This is Hassan's work. My dear generous friend has gone out into the marketplace and bought me another pair of slippers." He drew on the resplendent footwear and went home, thoroughly pleased with himself.

But what did the Cadi say, I wonder, when his servants, searching the dressing room for their master's slippers, brought him a tattered pair of objects that everybody recognized as belonging to Abu Kassem? The story is silent on this point. All we know is that he sent immediately for the culprit, fined him an enormous sum and restored to him his slippers.

Abu Kassem was sad at heart as he looked at the ragged objects. To have had to pay so much for so little! Well, at least they would give him no more trouble. He would get rid of the wretched things. So with a gesture of farewell he flung them into the River Tigris. "That," he thought, "is the end of them!" Alas and alack! Poor foolish man! Little did he know.

A few days later some fishermen discovered in their net two bundles of tattered leather. "Abu Kassem's slippers!" they said, and angrily hurled the offending footwear through Abu Kassem's window.

Down went the row of crystal bottles and up rose the scent of attar of roses as Abu Kassem's splendid bargains went crashing to the floor.

The miser was beside himself. He swept up the scattered glassy fragments and seized upon his slippers. "Wretches!" he cried. "This is enough! Ye shall do me no more harm." Thereupon he took a shovel, dug a hole in his tulip garden and buried his once-prized possessions.

"What can he be doing?" a neighbor asked, as he watched the laboring figure. "A rich man with so many servants about him to be digging in his own garden! He must be looking for hidden treasure. I will go and tell the Caliph!"

And since it was a law that hidden treasure belonged to the state, Abu Kassem soon found himself in court, standing before the governor. Where, he was asked, had he put the treasure? And when he protested that there was no treasure, that he had merely been burying his old slippers, the statement was received with laughter and general disbelief. The more he protested the more unlikely the story seemed—even to himself. Inevitably, he paid the fine and went home to unearth his slippers.

"The cursed things!" he cried in despair. "Shall I never rid myself of them?" He decided then to take the slippers out of the city, far from the sight of men. This he did. He hied him out into the country, dropped the offenders into a pond and breathed a sigh of relief. At last, he had seen the last of them!

But Fate had not finished with Abu Kassem. When he returned he discovered that the pond had been no pond but a reservoir, that the slippers had fouled the water pipes, that the workmen had recognized the slippers—how, indeed, could they help it?—and that he himself was to go to jail for stopping the city's water supply. So once again he paid a fine and once again he carried home his old unwanted possessions.

What was to be done? How could he free himself from his slippers and all their devil's tricks? Earth had refused them, so had water. What remained? Fire, of course! He would burn them to ashes. At the moment, however, they were still wet, so he put them out on the rooftop to dry.

There they lay, bleaching in the sun, till a dog on a nearby roof spied them, leapt the intervening space and snatched up the fatal slippers. He tossed them lightly into the air and down they fell to the street below where a woman was passing by. Now, it so happened that this woman was pregnant and the sudden blow on the top of her head made her slip and sprain her ankle. Her indignant husband, seeing how this had come about, ran to the judge and demanded payment. So Abu Kassem, now distraught, had once more to put his hand in his pocket.

But he cried, as he flung the money down and brandished the slippers aloft, "Lord judge, hear me! Be my witness. These slippers have been the bane of my life. Their tricks have reduced me to penury. Set me free from them, I implore thee! Let the evils that they bring in their train no longer be visited on my head. Of thy mercy, let this be enough!"

And the story relates that the Cadi, being a merciful man, heard the miser's plea, and relieved him of his slippers. But he counseled Abu Kassem, saying, "Hear, O Merchant, the voice of Wisdom. Nothing lasts forever, it says, and when a thing is no longer useful that thing should be relinquished."

Retold from the THAMARAT UL-AWRAK (*Fruit of Leaves*) of IBN HIJJAT AL-HAMAWI

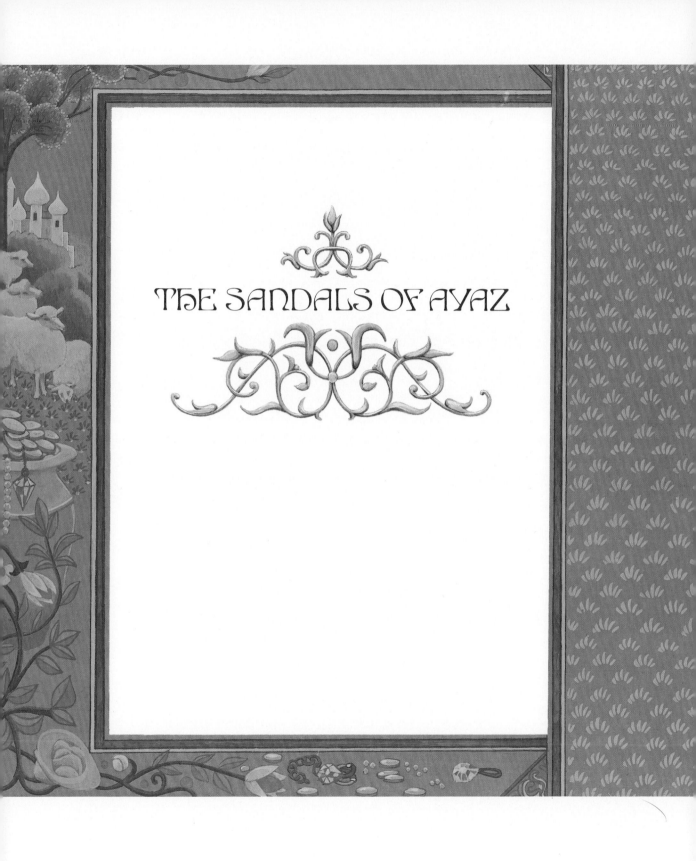

THE SANDALS OF AYAZ

LISTEN NOW TO THE STORY

of Ayaz, the Treasurer and trusted friend of the great King, Mahmoud. He was the first among all the courtiers and always stood at the King's right hand, clothed in a costly robe of honor.

You would never have thought to look at him that Ayaz had once been a shepherd boy, clad only in a sheepskin jacket and a pair of sandal shoon. But such was his good sense, his sagacity and his honesty that the King, hearing of it, first made him a member of his court and eventually put him in sole charge of all his most precious possessions.

From time to time in the course of his duties, Ayaz would bring his master a tally of all the gold and costly jewels that were stored in the palace cellars, and also of the divans and carpets that furnished the state apartments. But, strangely enough, of the contents of the modest chamber in the topmost tower he brought no tally at all. Indeed, he never mentioned them. Yet every day he climbed up to this little room and remained there for an hour. And every day, as he came out, he locked the iron door securely and put the key in his pocket. What lay behind that locked door was known to Ayaz alone.

Now, it so happened that on a particular occasion the King, deciding to put his courtiers to a test, entered the great hall of the council carrying a large, bright pearl. Smiling, he beckoned the Vizier and gave the pearl to him.

"Tell me," he said, "what this is worth."

"More than a hundred ass-loads of gold," the Vizier replied.

"Break it!" commanded King Mahmoud.

"Nay, how should I break it?" the Vizier cried. "How could I ruin this priceless thing?"

"Well said!" exclaimed the King, and presented the Vizier with a robe of honor.

Then he turned to the palace Chamberlain and handed him the pearl.

"What is this jewel worth?" he asked.

"Half a kingdom, may God preserve it!"

"Break it," commanded King Mahmoud.

"Alas, that would be a shameful deed! How could I be an enemy to the treasure house of the King?"

"Well said," the King exclaimed again. And he gave the Chamberlain a robe of honor and turned to the Minister of Justice. He, too, declined the task. How could he rob the treasury of such an inestimable jewel?

So it went on. Each courtier refused to break the pearl and to each the King gave a costly garment. Unfortunate men! How was it that they could not guess that they were being put on trial?

Last of all came the turn of Ayaz.

"Tell me, my friend, what this pearl is worth!"

"More," said Ayaz, "than I can say."

"Break it!" commanded King Mahmoud.

Now, it so happened that Ayaz, by a lucky chance, had two stones hid in his sleeve. And without a moment's hesitation he crushed the pearl between the stones and so reduced it to dust.

The courtiers all rose up in protest. "Whoever breaks such a perfect thing is an infidel!" they cried.

"Not so!" said Ayaz, bowing to them. "Answer, O princes, one simple question! What is more precious to your hearts—the pearl or the King's command? Is he not lacking in true wisdom who puts a mere jewel before the word of the King? When I look for radiance, I turn my gaze to him alone."

At that the courtiers bowed their heads. Shame and terror filled their hearts. "Alas," they cried, "we are undone! We have been deflected from the path of truth by the grandeur of a worldly bauble. Our fate is sealed. We shall lose our heads."

"So!" said the King—and now he frowned. "For the sake of this paltry thing from the sea, my command has been held contemptible." And he made a sign to the Executioner, who drew his sword from its scabbard.

But Ayaz, full of boundless love, prostrated himself before the throne. "O King, from whom comes every fortune, grant them, as a boon, their lives. Do not banish them from thy presence. Thy pardon itself will teach them wisdom."

"So be it, then," said King Mahmoud, and for love of Ayaz reprieved them all.

The courtiers breathed a sigh of relief. They had been given back their lives. But anger, not gratitude, filled their hearts. And, as the fox is to the lion, so were they to Ayaz.

For day after day, as they watched him climbing to his secret turret, they plotted against him.

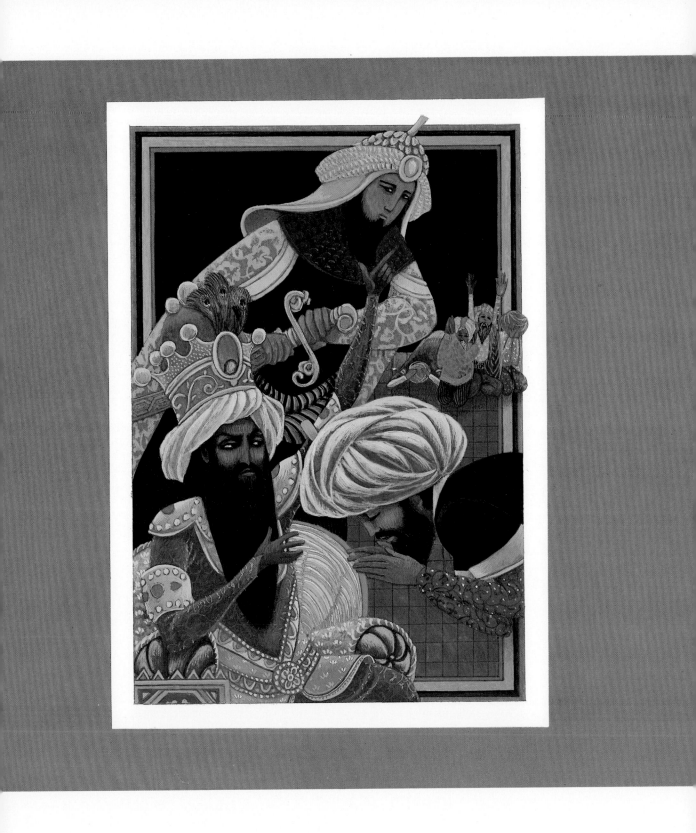

"What," they asked, whispering scandal, "has he hidden there in the uppermost chamber? He alone keeps the key and brings the King no tally. Is he not Treasurer to the palace? Without doubt he is hoarding gold and keeping a precious store for himself. It is right that we tell the King."

So they did that, rejoicing in their hearts that now they would be revenged on Ayaz.

And the King wondered. "What has my servant concealed from me?"

And he gave orders to a certain Amir, saying, "Go at midnight, when Ayaz is asleep, force the door of the uppermost chamber and whatever you find is yours."

Now, the King had no evil thoughts of Ayaz. He was once again putting the courtiers on trial. Nevertheless, his heart misgave him lest the charge be true and his servant shamed.

"He has not done this thing," he mused. "And if he has, there is reason in it. Let Ayaz do whatever he will, for he is my beloved. I would need a mouth as broad as heaven to praise him as he deserves." Thus he thought within himself.

And meanwhile the courtiers went to work. They struck at the door of the uppermost chamber and broke the iron lock. Then they swarmed in, jostling each other, greedily seeking for hidden treasure.

They looked to the right. They looked to the left. Up and down and round they looked. But the little uppermost chamber was empty, except for a dusty sheepskin jacket and a pair of tattered sandals.

"Bring picks and shovels!" the courtiers cried. Thereupon they began to dig, making holes in the walls and floor. And the holes themselves seemed to cry against them, "Behold, O men, we are empty."

The fact, indeed, could not be denied. No treasure lay in the uppermost chamber and the courtiers went to the King next morning, pale-faced and ashamed.

"What—empty-handed?" the King asked, slyly. "Surely you should be heavy-laden. Come! Show me the hoarded gold and jewels that my faithful friend has stolen."

"O King of the world," they cried. "Forgive! We have nothing to show thee but a sheepskin jacket and a pair of sandal shoon."

"Nay!" said the King. "In this case it is not I who deal with punishment or forgiveness. That right belongs to my faithful servant. What dost thou say, Ayaz?"

Ayaz stepped forward.

"O King," he said, "the command is thine. Thou art the sun. I am less than a star. But let me remind thee on their behalf that if I had neglected jacket and shoon, if I had not secreted myself behind the door of the uppermost chamber, I should not have roused in them suspicion nor sown the seeds of envy."

"I shall note it," answered King Mahmoud. "But, O Ayaz, tell me this. Why these marks of affection for a rustic shoe? Thou hast mingled much of thy soul's love with two old articles of dress, and kept them both in a special closet. Why accord them such dignity?"

"It is fit that I do so," said Ayaz. "I was low on the earth and thou lifted me up. From my tent thou hast brought me to marble halls. I know that all this eminence is but a gift of thine. And without this gift, what am I?"

"A shepherd boy!" sneered the courtiers.

"True," said Ayaz, "a keeper of sheep, with nothing but a sheepskin jacket and a pair of sandal shoon. Yet these things, O King, O princes, teach me how to know myself! And he who knows himself knows God. The seed from which I come is my shoon, my blood is the sheepskin jacket. Therefore, in the uppermost chamber I commune with my beginnings. 'Do not regard thy present greatness,' the sheepskin jacket tells me. 'Remember,' say the sandal shoon, 'the lowliness of thy birth.' So I keep them, O Master, to remind me. That is all my secret."

Ayaz bowed low before the throne.

"All honor to thy sandal shoon," cried the King, raising him up. "Keep them, O Friend, forever by thee. For I see that they are thy chiefest treasure."

And thus it was that the wise Ayaz, faithful to his original self, preserved his tattered sandals.

Retold from THE MATHNAWÍ OF JALÁLU'DDIN RÚMÍ

ABOUT THE BOOK

The paintings for *Two Pairs of Shoes*
were prepared in gouache on paper.
The decorative borders were also created
by the artists. The art was then
camera-separated and printed in five colors.
The text type is 14-point Aldine
Bembo Monotype, and the display
is Typositor Edd Solid.